Ben's Trumpet

by RACHEL ISADORA

Angus & Robertson · Publishers

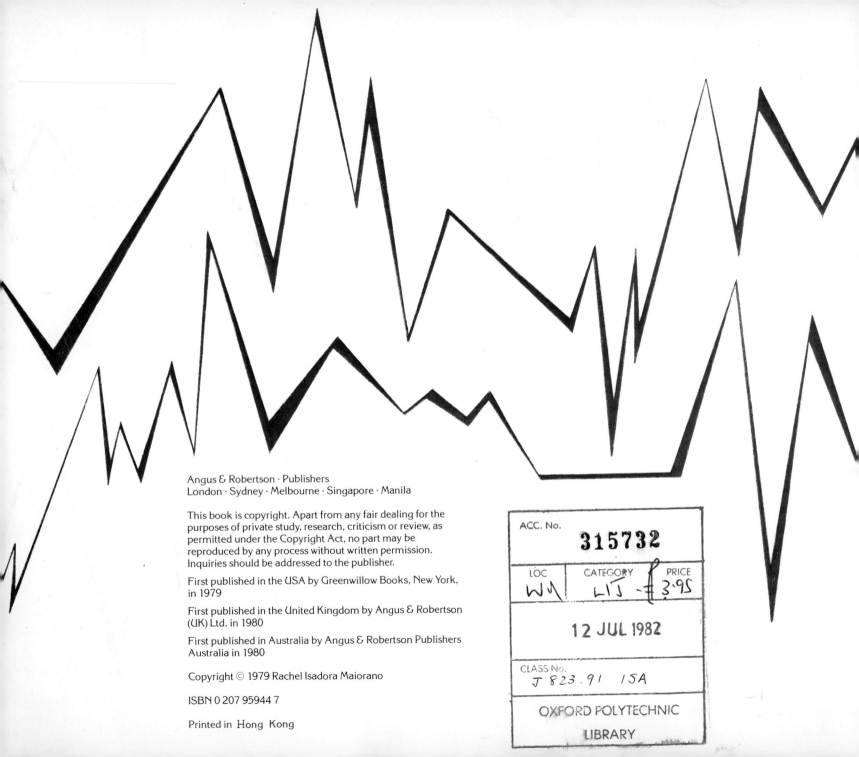

Angus & Robertson · Publishers
London · Sydney · Melbourne · Singapore · Manila

First published in the USA by Greenwillow Books, New York,
in 1979

First published in the United Kingdom by Angus & Robertson
(UK) Ltd. in 1980

First published in Australia by Angus & Robertson Publishers
Australia in 1980

Copyright © 1979 Rachel Isadora Maiorano

ISBN 0 207 95944 7

Printed in Hong Kong

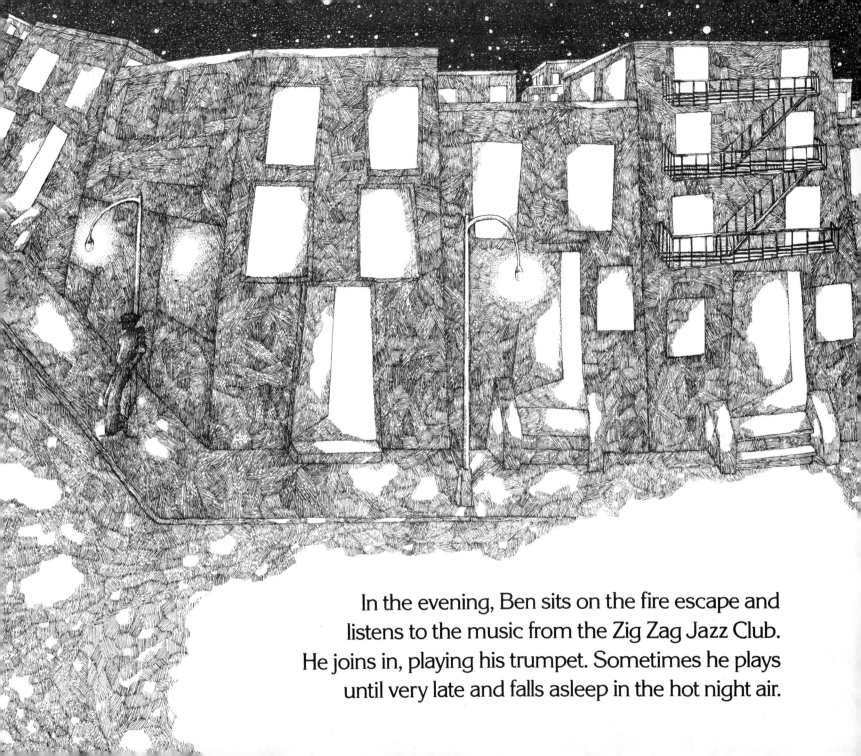

In the evening, Ben sits on the fire escape and
listens to the music from the Zig Zag Jazz Club.
He joins in, playing his trumpet. Sometimes he plays
until very late and falls asleep in the hot night air.

Every day on the way home from school,
Ben stops by the Zig Zag Jazz Club.

He watches the musicians practise.

The pianist,

the saxophonist,

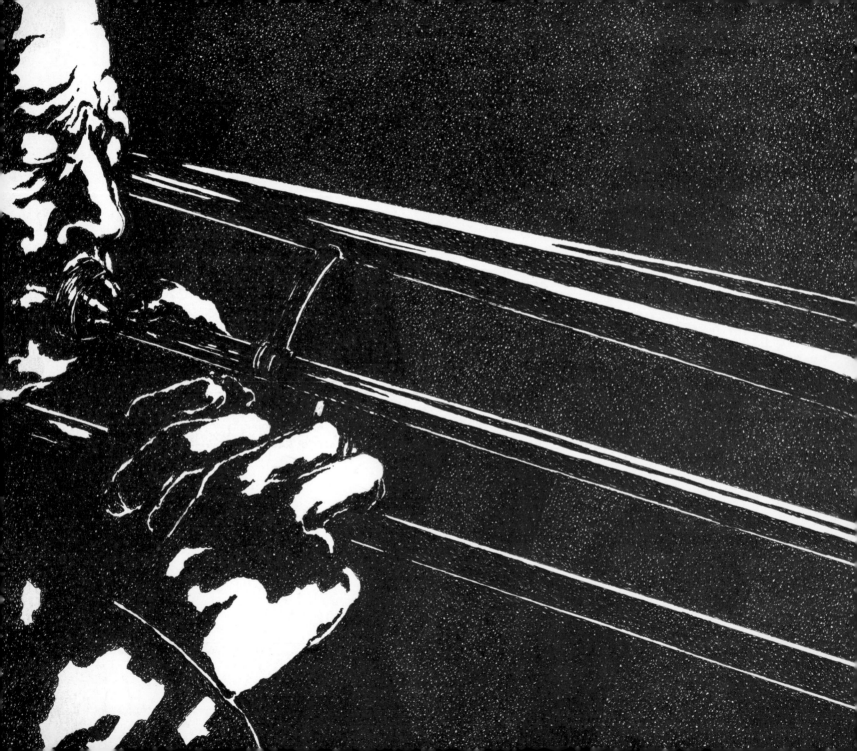

the trombonist,

and the drummer.

But most of all Ben thinks the trumpeter
is the cat's meow.

Ben feels the rhythm of the
music all the way home.

He plays for his mama,
grandmother and
baby brother.

And for his papa and his friends.

One day, Ben is sitting on the steps
and playing his trumpet.
"I like your horn," someone says.

It is the trumpeter from the Zig Zag Jazz Club!
Ben smiles and watches him walk to the Club.

The next day, after school, Ben stops and listens
to the musicians practising a red hot piece.
He starts blasting away at his trumpet.
Some kids in front of the store watch him.
"Hey, what ya doing?" they yell.

Ben stops and turns around.
"What ya think ya doing?" they ask again.
"I'm playing my trumpet," Ben answers.
"Man, you're crazy! You got no trumpet!"
They laugh and laugh.

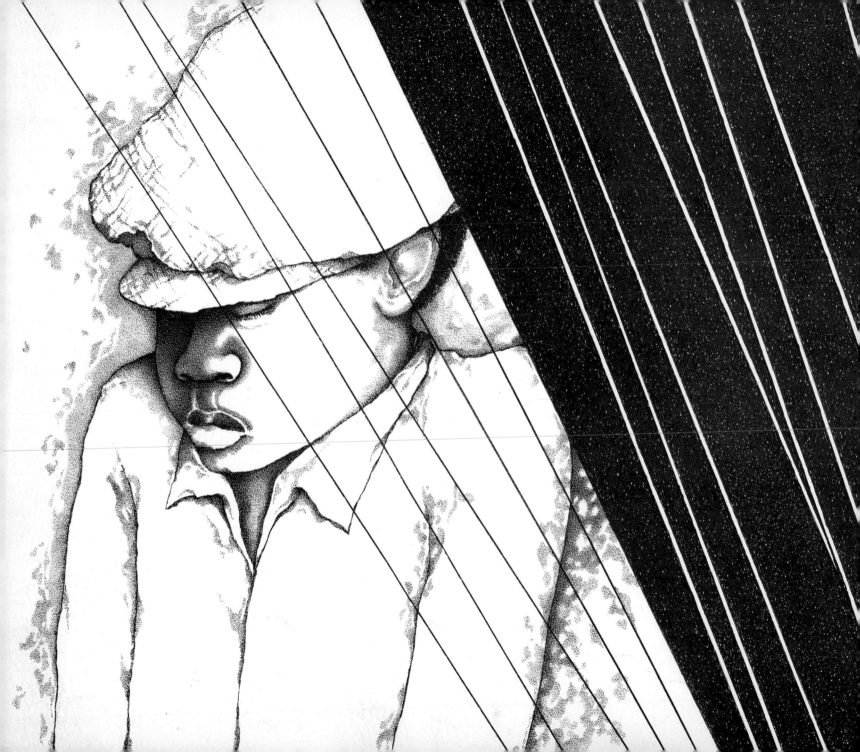

Ben puts his hands in his pockets
and walks slowly home.

He sits on the steps and watches the blinking lights of the
Zig Zag Jazz Club. He sits there a long time, just watching.

Down the street the band comes out for a break.
The trumpeter comes over to Ben.
"Where's your horn?" he asks.
"I don't have one," Ben says.
The trumpeter puts his hand on Ben's shoulder.
"Come on over to the club," he says,

"and we'll see what we can do."

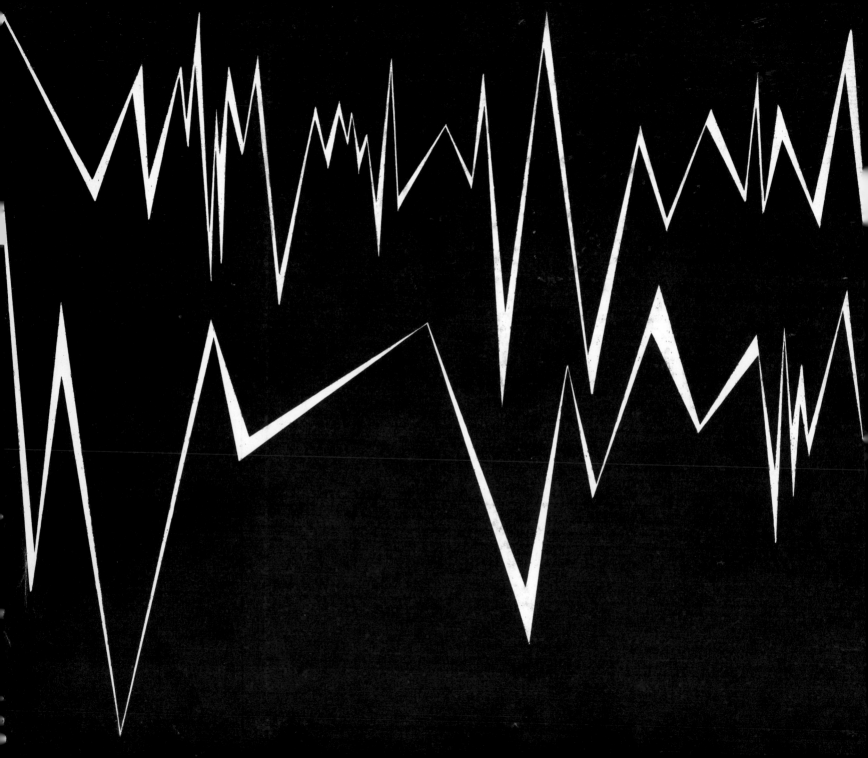